This edition published by Parragon Inc. in 2013

Parragon Inc.
440 Park Avenue South, 13th Floor
New York, NY 10016
www.parragon.com

ISBN 978-1-4723-3133-5

Printed in China

Beauty
and the
the Beast

Retold by Anne Marie Ryan

Illustrated by Jacqueline East

PaRRagon

Bath · New York · Singapore · Hong Kong · Cologne · Delhi
Melbourne · Amsterdam · Johannesburg · Shenzhen

Once upon a time, there was a rich merchant who lived in a big house with his three daughters.

All three girls were beautiful, but only the youngest daughter, Beauty, was loving and kind. Her older sisters were nasty and selfish, and cared only for jewels and fancy clothes.

One day, there was a huge storm.
Lightning flashed and waves crashed.

The merchant's ship was lost at sea,
along with all the cargo it was carrying.

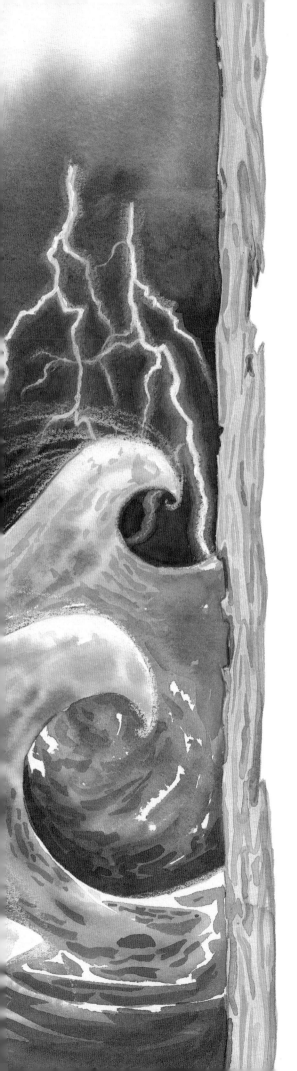

The merchant and his family were now so poor that they had to trade their grand house for a little cottage.

Many months later, to the merchant's relief, his ship arrived back in port. Before hurrying off to fetch his silks and spices, he asked his daughters what they wanted him to bring back.

"Bring me some satin clothes," the eldest daughter demanded.

"A diamond necklace would be quite nice, I suppose," the middle daughter said.

"If you please, Father, I would love a single red rose," Beauty asked politely.

But when the merchant arrived, he found that the ship's cargo had been taken to pay his debts. There would be no presents after all.

Trudging home through the forest, the
merchant got lost. As night fell, he came
upon a palace and decided to ask for shelter.

KNOCK!

KNOCK!

KNOCK!

The merchant rapped on the door, but no one seemed to be home.

He pushed open the heavy door and peered inside.

There, much to his delight, he found a table laden with a feast!

Zzzzzz ... Zzzzzz ... Zzzzzz

After eating his fill, the weary merchant climbed into a soft bed and fell sound asleep.

The next morning, the merchant set off for home. As he walked through the palace gardens, a heavenly fragrance floated on the breeze.

Following the scent, the merchant found a beautiful rose bush in full bloom. Remembering Beauty's wish, he snipped off one perfect red blossom.

Just then, a **horrible, hairy beast** reared up next to him!

"You ate my food and slept in my bed, now you steal my roses. You shall die!"

The merchant begged for forgiveness.
"It … it … it is for my daughter," he explained.

The beast agreed to let the
merchant go, but ordered him to
send his daughter to the palace.

When the merchant returned home, the eldest daughters were angry because he hadn't brought them any presents.

"Humph!" they said, flouncing off.

Beauty hugged her father tight. "Oh, how pretty!" she exclaimed when he gave her the rose. She buried her face in the soft petals and breathed in its sweet perfume.

But when she looked up, she saw that her father was weeping.
"What's wrong, Father?" Beauty asked.

The merchant sadly explained what had happened,
and Beauty bravely agreed to visit the beast.

Early the next morning, Beauty left
her home and set off toward the palace.

She knocked softly on the palace door.

Tap! Tap! Tap!

Beauty shrank back in fright when the fearsome beast appeared. But the beast bowed low, took her hand, and showed her to a room filled with roses.

"Here, you will have everything your heart desires," he said, and Beauty felt her fears melt away.

Beauty soon grew very fond of the beast, for he was always kind to her.

One day, while they strolled in the gardens, the beast asked, **"Will you marry me?"** But Beauty said no. That night, she dreamed she was walking through the garden with a prince.

The beast tried again another day. While he and Beauty ate a delicious dinner, the beast asked, **"Will you marry me?"** Again, Beauty answered no. That night, she dreamed she was dining with a prince.

The beast did not give up. As he and Beauty waltzed through the ballroom, the beast asked, **"Will you marry me?"** Once more, Beauty replied no. That night, she dreamed she was dancing with a prince.

Beauty began to wonder whether the beast was hiding the handsome prince from her dreams in the palace.

She searched everywhere ...

... from the highest

tower to the

lowest dungeon.

But she could
not find the prince
anywhere!

Although the beast had become her friend, Beauty missed her father very much. She begged the beast to let her visit him.

"You may leave, but return to me in one week." He handed her a magic mirror. "This will show you what's happening at the palace," he said. Then he slipped a ring on her dainty finger. "And this will take you back here if you twist it three times."

Beauty thanked the beast, and later that day, she left the palace and ran all the way home.

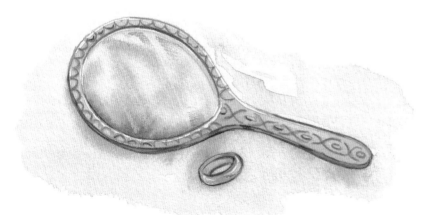

Beauty was overjoyed to see her father! She told him all about the palace and the beast, and how he was gentle and good.

Her father was so pleased to hear that the beast had been kind to Beauty, but her sisters were jealous of her elegant dresses and sparkling jewels.

The sisters decided to trick Beauty.

"Please don't go back to the palace—we'll miss you so much!"

they pleaded, pretending to cry.

They secretly hoped the beast would get angry that she was late and gobble Beauty up!

When the week had passed, Beauty decided to stay at home. But even though she loved spending time with her father, she couldn't stop worrying about her friend. She knew he would be missing her.

She gazed into the magic mirror and was shocked by what she saw. The poor beast was lying by the rose bush, dying from a broken heart!

Beauty twisted the ring ...

one, two, three
times.

In an instant, she was by the beast's side. Beauty held her friend and cried,

"Oh, please don't die—if you do, so will I!"

As Beauty's tears fell on the beast, he became the handsome prince from her dreams!

He told her that long ago a witch had turned him into a beast because he denied her shelter. Only true love could break the spell!

The prince asked Beauty to marry him, and this time she said . . . YES!

The End